The Royal Muddle

Michael Rosen

Illustrated by
Colin West

Young Piper Books
in association with Macmillan Children's Books

The search was on, the new Queen had to be found . . .
In the Operations Room, the Librarian spread out the ancient manuscripts, maps, charts and doner kebabs.

"She won't know she's a Queen," said the Librarian.

It may come as a big shock to her and her friends. People will be amazed that there, in the heart of their little town, in a damp patch not much bigger than a roof-rack, lives the frog who is to be our queen!

The Advisers thanked the Librarian for all the work she had done, and sent her off to the little place in the mountains with the two televisions.

To the little place in the mountains with two televisions

"Right," said Lord Spoke, "we need a map-reader, an explorer, a cook, a royal announcer and a wet patch about the size of a roof-rack."
"They must be sent for," said Lady Leg.

A few minutes later they arrived. "Introduce yourselves," said Lord Ear, a quiet man.

Lord Spoke spoke.

"Thank you," said the Expedition
Party Leader, Map-Reader Sentfor,
and they left forthwith.

They followed the map to the traffic lights and turned left. Just as they did so, a voice called out from the lunch basket.

And out popped Lord Doner Kebab who had hidden in there, which was a dangerous thing to do with a name like that.

So they turned right and arrived at a damp patch that was the size of a roof-rack. The Map-Reader started calling out in a soft voice.

After 34 hours of this, she was getting quite tired.

The local people were becoming
quite curious by now.

However, they soon found out.

Suddenly there was a shout, a
victorious cry, a whoop of delight,
and a shriek:

IT'S THE QUEEN! IT'S THE QUEEN!

Yes, a frog had hopped into view.

This must be the new Queen
of this great country of ours!

They all bowed low, which was quite
difficult because they were all
crawling along the ground.

"Quick, Announcer, announce it,"
said the Map-Reader.
"Oh People," said the Announcer,
"this is our new Queen. Long live the
Queen."

clapping, hoping that the
little group crowding round the goal
area would get off the football pitch
because their team was playing the
cupholders and the kick off was
being held up by all this royal stuff.

The good Queen had begun her reign.

Of course, there was a coronation,
which was shown on television . . .

An artist came to do the royal
painting of her,

a poet wrote a poem about her

and some flies came and got eaten by her.

The poet's poem went like this:

You may not
be big,
In fact you are
quite small,
But we all know
You're the great-
est frog of all.
Oh yes, Oh yes,
Oh yes!

The newspapers loved her and were full of stories about what she was wearing and lots of gossipy things about nice young men frogs who were sometimes seen hopping about.

She was very popular with the crowds wherever she went, like when she had to open a new bowling alley,

or launch a new ship.

In the evenings over tea, people would chat about her.

Sometimes the Queen
went on Royal Tours.

The whole story was running like a
fairy tale until one day, out of the
blue, a dark cloud came to spoil
things.

The new Librarian at the Royal Records Office spent many, many hours poring over the old records. In fact he spent so long, he poured all sorts of things over the Royal Records. One night, late, he suddenly came across an old, old manuscript.

He dashed off to the Royal Huddle
Room to speak to the Royal Huddle.

The Royal Huddle gasped.

"You mean . . . you mean . . . " said
Lord Spoke, "our Queen is just a
frog? Oh no. This is awful."
There were gasps and sighs and sobs
all round the room.

So the Queen was invited to the
Royal Huddle Room and the
Announcer shouted at her:

But the Queen took no notice at all.

The Announcer broke down sobbing.

I'm only trying to do my job!
I've got a wife and fifteen
children to support!
Doesn't anyone care about me?
I've never been a troublemaker...

He was taken out and put to bed
with a hot water bottle and a nice
book to read before being put in
prison for being
a trouble-maker.

The Royal Huddle considered the
problem:

...And he could easily be put in prison too...

...So the obvious thing is NOT TELL ANYONE ABOUT IT!

Then no one in the country will know she's just a frog!

And so life went on as before. The Queen went on opening festivals,

visiting foreign countries and having holidays in beautiful places . . .

Titles in the FLIPPERS series

Now flip the book over
to read
THE ROYAL HUDDLE

Now flip the book over
to read
THE ROYAL MUDDLE

And this they did.

"How nice," said Lady Leg. "Let me speak to her."
Lady Leg picked up the phone.

Lord Also-Spoke turned to the rest.

She rushed off to find the Royal Advisers but found they had all gone to the little place in the mountains and were busy watching two televisions.

She got on the phone to them straight away.

Librarian Sentfor went off to the Royal Records Office and went through the Royal Records. She was at it for days.

She unrolled scrolls,

she deciphered manuscripts,

and she unearthed long-lost doner kebabs.

Finally, she found what she had been looking for.

"We have work for you, Librarian," said Lady Leg. "You have to go through the Royal Records."

"Were you ever a doctor?" said Lord Spoke inquisitively.

"Yes," said the Librarian.

"And *where* were you a doctor?" said Lord Spoke, before he was spoken to.

Here, you old dolt, about three minutes ago. But on the way out I applied for a job as a librarian, and after a long interview and a few days work experience, I got it.

Well done!

Now who was going to be next in
line for the throne?
"Send for the Librarian," said Lord
Doner Kebab. ✶
The Librarian arrived forthwith.

FOOT ✶ Lord Doner Kebab, like Lord Sandwich
NOTE: before him, has given his name to a
well-known snack Facts like this win
good marks on quiz shows, you know.

So the Messenger told the Announcer
and the Announcer told the People
and the People said, "Oh no, poor
Old King Joseph is dead again.
Twice in a week," and they had a
funeral.

R.I.P
AGAIN

So off she went to the mountains.

"Right, Messenger, you know what
to do," said Lord Not-Before-
Breakfast – who, as you've guessed,
has not said much so far in this story
because everything that's happened
so far has happened before
breakfast.

So the Announcer went back to the Messenger and the Messenger went back to the Royal Huddle Room.

Lord Also-Spoke looked up from his sausages.

"Look, I don't want to know. I've got a wife and six kids to support, I can't risk being put in prison or being thrown into a pit of snakes."

"OK, mate, don't you worry about it," said someone. "But just to keep you informed – the King…is…dead."

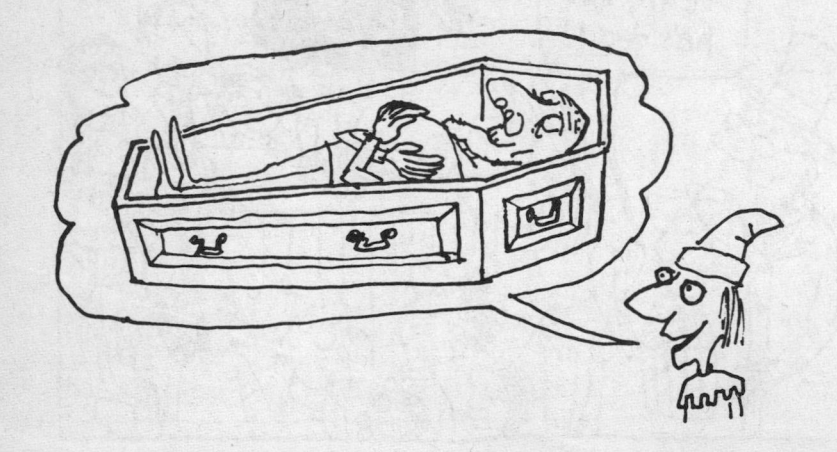

"What's so funny?" said the Announcer. "I'm only doing my job. I've got a wife and three kids to support. You don't know how hard it is to make all these announcements."

Someone explained.

At that, all the People burst out laughing.

In the Royal Huddle Room, the
Advisers talked to the Doctor.
"What shall we announce today?"

So the Messenger told the Announcer
and the Announcer told the People.

One of the doctors had sat on the bowl of grapes and, as bad luck would have it, it wasn't one of the doctors in a *long* white coat but one of the doctors in a *short* white coat.

The Nurse had kindly covered up Old King Joseph and made arrangements. *

FOOT NOTE:

* You might wonder what sort of arrangements, but that's just what we say when we don't want to SAY what sort of arrangements. Clever, isn't it?

Meanwhile, at Old King Joseph's bedside, there was a problem: they had put the bowl of grapes, the twenty Get Well Soon cards, the two doctors in short white coats and the three doctors in long white coats *in* the oxygen tent.

So Lady Leg told the Messenger and
the Messenger told the Announcer
and the Announcer told the People.

Doctor Sentfor rushed in to see the King. She soon knew what to do.

Panic broke out in the Royal Huddle Room.

"Is this the right man for the job?"
said Lady Leg.
"She's not a man," said Lord Spoke.
Just then the Nurse rushed in.

"We want to keep Old King Joseph alive," said Lady Leg.

"Yes, ma'am," said Doctor Sentfor.

"When?"

"Now, you clot," said Lord Spoke unkindly. "It will be too late tomorrow."

What was going to happen?

The Royal Advisers got into a huddle
in the Royal Huddle Room.
"Perhaps he can be kept alive," said
Lady Leg.
"Splendid, let's do it," said Lord
Spoke. "Send for the doctor."
The doctor was sent for.

Old King Joseph was dying.
He was so old – 432 years old, in
fact – that there was no one left alive
who could be king or queen. He had
no sons, daughters, wives or
husbands. He had no fathers or
mothers. He had lost his mother and
father years ago and hadn't found
any new ones.